# Not Yet, Rose

With love and gratitude for my parents, Deane and Judy Leonard,
who gave me the chance to be a little sister and a big sister
and taught me what love and family are all about.
I'm so glad I came to your house!
You are the best.
– S.L.H.

To Thomas Bergstra
– N.R.

Text © 2009 Susanna Leonard Hill
Illustrations © 2009 Nicole Rutten

Published in 2009 by Eerdmans Books for Young Readers
an imprint of Wm. B. Eerdmans Publishing Co.

Wm. B. Eerdmans Publishing Co.
2140 Oak Industrial Dr. NE, Grand Rapids, Michigan 49505
P.O. Box 163, Cambridge CB3 9PU U.K.

www.eerdmans.com/youngreaders

Manufactured in Singapore

14 13 12 11 10 09   9 8 7 6 5 4 3 2 1

Library of Congress Cataloging-in-Publication Data

Hill, Susanna Leonard.
Not yet, Rose / by Susanna Leonard Hill ; illustrated by Nicole Rutten.
p. cm.
Summary: While impatiently waiting for the birth of a new baby brother or sister,
Rose imagines the things they will do together and how her life will change.
ISBN 978-0-8028-5326-4
[1. Babies — Fiction. 2. Brothers and sisters — Fiction. 3. Imagination — Fiction.]
I. Rutten, Nicole, ill. II. Title.
PZ7.H55743No 2008
[E]—dc22
2008031736

Type set in Angie.
Illustrations created with watercolor and pencil.

# Not Yet, Rose

written by Susanna Leonard Hill
illustrated by Nicole Rutten

Eerdmans Books for Young Readers
Grand Rapids, Michigan • Cambridge, U.K.

On Monday, Rose wanted a sister. She
raced into her parents' room.
"Is the baby here yet?" she asked.
"Not yet, Rose," said her mother.

"If I had a sister," Rose said, "we could play dress-up and read stories and sing *Way Down South Where Bananas Grow*."

"You could do that with a brother, too," said her father.

"A sister is more the same," said Rose. "A sister would be like me."

But then she got to thinking about it. Maybe a sister would be too much the same.

On Tuesday, Rose wanted a brother.
"Is the baby here yet?" she asked,
skipping into the kitchen.

"Not yet, Rose," said her father. He
gave her a kiss and left for work.

Rose munched her toast and sipped her milk.

"If I had a brother," she said, "we could put a blanket and a picnic and some fishing poles in my red wagon and go fishing down at the pond."

"You could do that with a sister, too," her mother said.

"A brother would be better," said Rose, "because a brother would be different."

"Different from what?" asked her mother.

"Different from me," said Rose.

"The baby will be different from you whether it's a boy or a girl," said her mother. "No one else can be Rose."

That was true, Rose thought. She was the only Rose. Still, once the baby came, she would not be the only one.

By Wednesday morning, Rose had decided that she didn't want a baby at all. She thumped slowly down the stairs in her bunny slippers.

"Is the baby here yet?" she asked her mother.

"Not yet, Rose," said her mother.

"What do you need a baby for anyway?" asked Rose. "You've already got me."

"If there's no baby," said her mother, "how can you be the big sister?"

Well, thought Rose, being the big sister *was* an important job. Still . . .

"What if I don't like being a big sister?" she asked.

"You won't know until you try," said her mother. "But I think you'll like it."

Rose thought about it. Her mother might be right, but it still sounded like trouble.

On Thursday morning, Rose went into the bathroom to help her father shave.

"Is the baby here yet?" she asked.

"Not yet, Rose," said her father. He dabbed some shaving cream on her face.

"Will the baby shave with us?" asked Rose.

"Sure," said her father. "But not right away. The baby will be too little. Shaving is something you have to grow into."

"What will the baby do?" asked Rose.

"Not much," said her father. "New babies mostly need to be held and rocked and sung to."

"That stuff's boring," said Rose.

"Not to a baby," said her father.

"Well, it doesn't sound like fun to me." Rose was beginning to wonder about this whole baby thing. "I'm not sure a baby is such a good idea," she told her father. "I don't think we should have one after all."

Her father laughed. "You were a baby once," he said. "And look how well you turned out."

Well, thought Rose, that was certainly true!

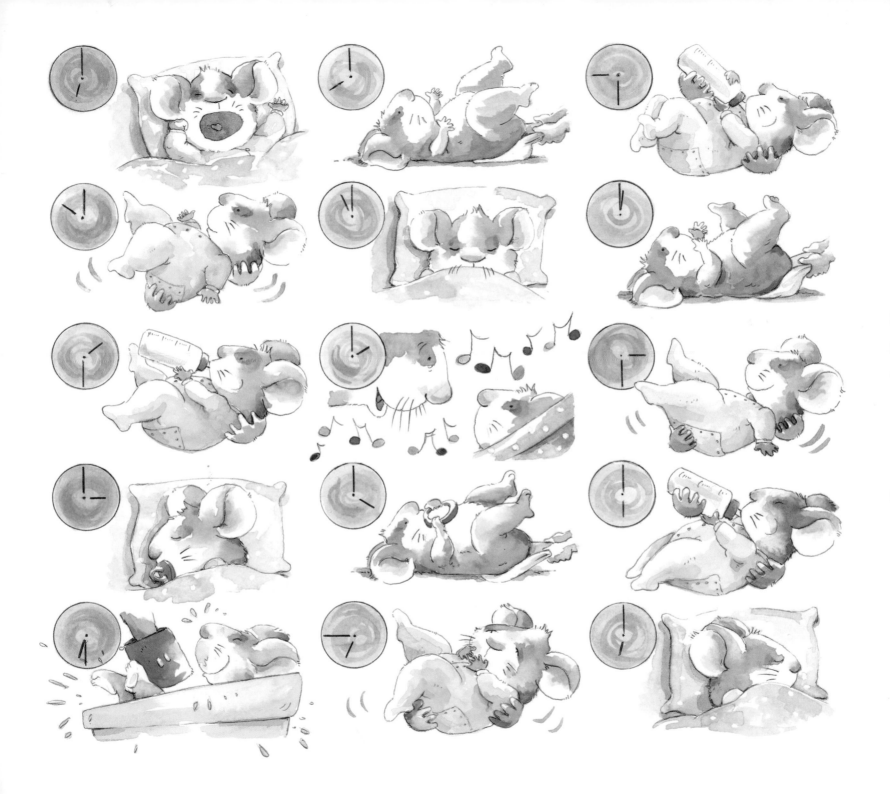

On Friday morning when Rose woke up, her parents weren't home. Grandma and Grandpa were there.

"Mommy and Daddy are at the hospital. You have a baby brother!" said Grandma. "Isn't that nice?"

"I don't know," said Rose. "I haven't seen him yet. When can we go?"

"Not yet, Rose," said Grandpa. "But I'll make pancakes to celebrate, and in a little while your dad will take you to see him."

### Recipe for pancakes

1 ¼ cup flour
3 teaspoons baking powder
1 tablespoon sugar
2 tablespoons oil
Pinch of salt
1 beaten egg
1 cup milk

Mix ingredients together in a bowl. Pour or scoop batter onto a greased frying pan or griddle, using approximately ¼ cup for each pancake. Flip when bubbles start to appear. Serve hot with maple syrup. Makes 10 to 12 pancakes.

Soon after breakfast, Rose's father came home. She
ran to greet him, and he swung her up high in the air.

"Want to go see your mom and meet your brother?"
he asked.

"Okay," said Rose.

Rose had a lot on her mind. She was a big sister
now. What if she wasn't a good big sister? What if she
didn't like her new brother? What if he didn't like her?
Rose was very quiet all the way to the hospital.

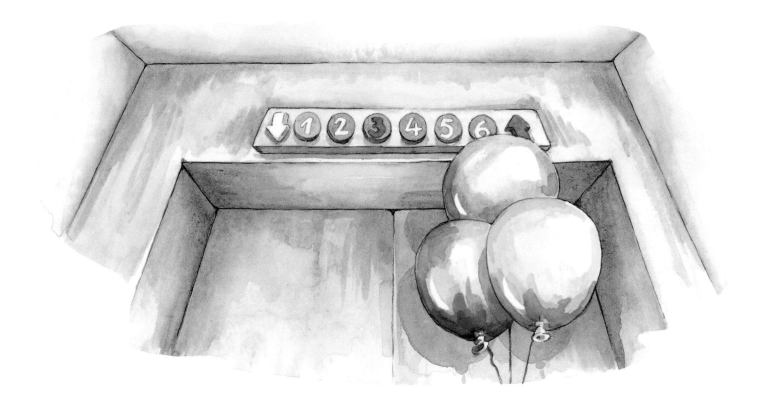

When they got to the hospital, they went up an
elevator and along a quiet white hall. The lights were
very bright and it smelled funny. Rose walked close
to her father and held his hand.

"Where's Mommy?" she asked.

"Right here," said her father.

Rose walked into a room with a big window and a bed. Her mother sat on the bed with a small blue bundle in her arms.

"Hi, Sweetie," she said with a smile. Rose ran to her and gave her a hug. "This is your brother Luke."

Rose looked at the small rosy face. The baby's eyes were closed.

"He has no eyebrows!" she said.

Her mother laughed. "You didn't either when you were born," she said. "Don't worry. They'll grow."

"Boy," said Rose. "He sure is small."

The baby squirmed and opened his eyes. They were blue, just like Rose's. His tiny mouth stretched wide in a huge yawn. He looked so funny that Rose laughed.

"Would you like to hold him?" asked her mother.

"Okay," said Rose.

She climbed up on the bed very carefully.

Then she sat in her mother's lap, and held the baby on her lap.

"Hi, Luke," she said to her baby brother. "I'm your big sister, Rose."

She reached out a finger and touched his tiny hand. To her surprise, he grabbed it tightly.

"Look!" Rose said. "He's holding my hand!"

She rocked him gently and very softly she sang, *Way Down South Where Bananas Grow.*

This wasn't so bad. One of these days, she thought, we'll play dress-up and go fishing. But her father had been right. Holding and rocking and singing were just right for now.

Luke's eyes closed again. Rose felt his warm little body grow heavy with sleep. It was a nice feeling. Suddenly, she was glad he was here.

"Are your arms getting tired, Rose?" her mother asked. "Do you want to put him down?"

"Not yet," said Rose.